TOBY TO THE RESCUE

Leo Donaldson

✱✱✱✱✱

✱✱✱✱✱

Please note that I use English-(South African) spelling throughout. You will see doubled letters (focussed), ou's (colour) and 're' (centre) as well as a few other differences from American spelling.

✱✱✱✱✱

Toby to the rescue

This book is dedicated to my wonderful children,
Jean-Luc and Jess-Leigh, and to Jethro who,
sadly, will never have the joy of reading it.

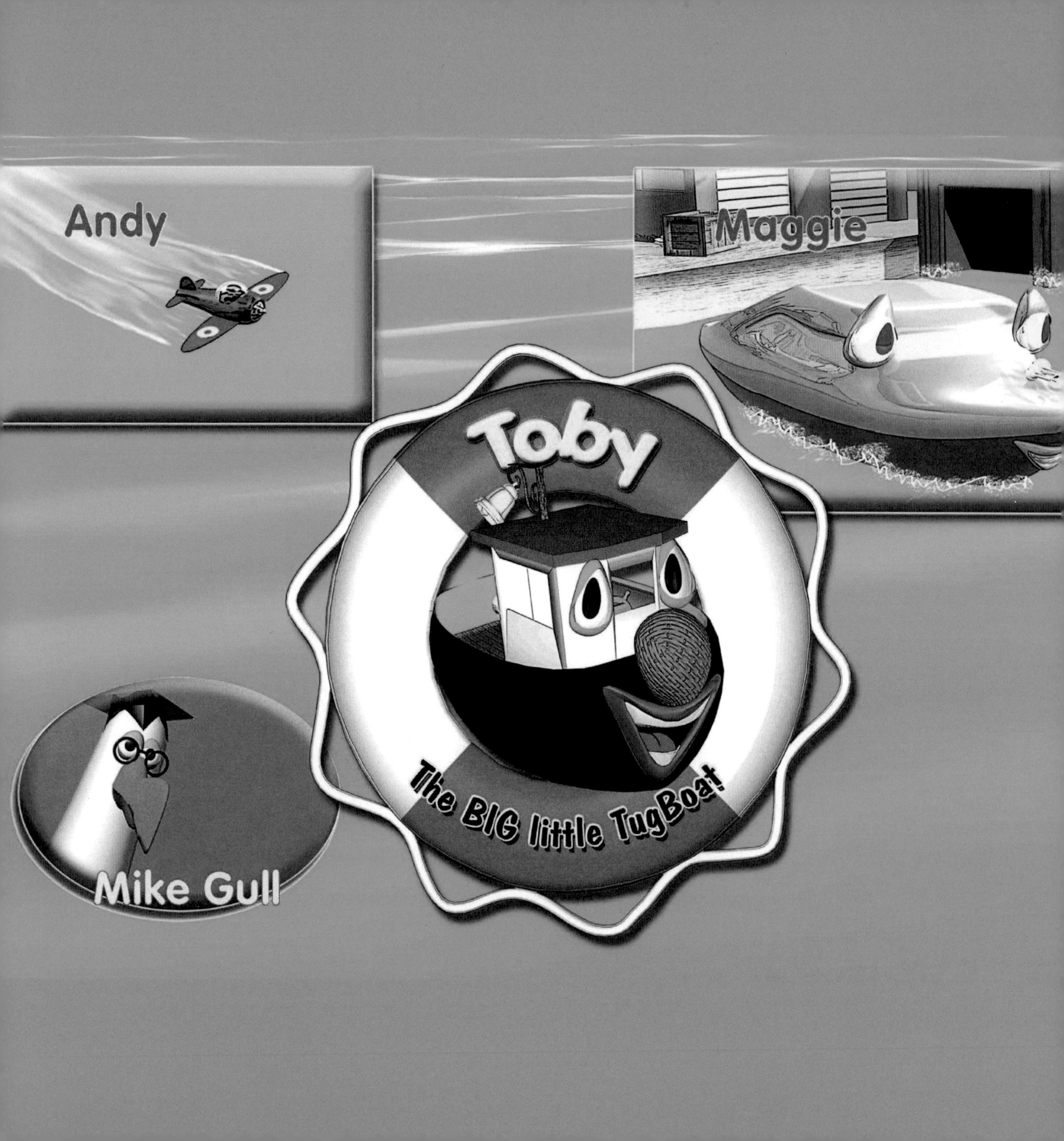
Andy
Maggie
Toby
The BIG little TugBoat
Mike Gull

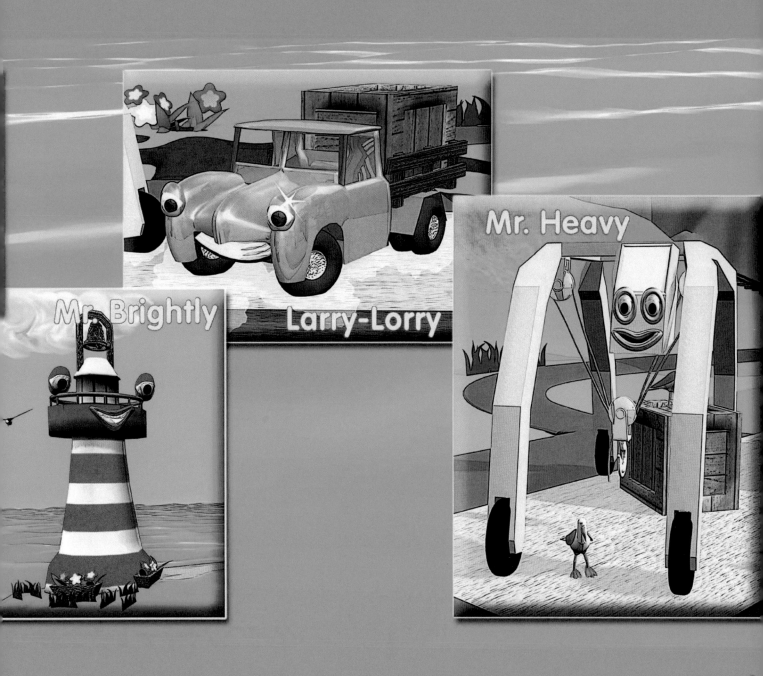

'Rise and Shine! Rise and Shine!' squawk the seagulls from

the rooftops of Kalk Bay harbour.

'Ah, good morning, my gull friends,' beams

Mr. Heavy the harbour crane.

Although Larry-Lorry is excited about going to Cape Town,

he is worried about the large crate that

Mr. Heavy is struggling to load onto

his back.

'You'll have to move, huh …

closer, Larry,' pants Mr. Heavy.

Hello, kids.
How many crates
do you think Larry-
Lorry will be able
to carry?

'Okay,' mutters Larry, reversing carefully to stop directly beneath the crate.

'Thanks, Larry. Phew, that's quite a weight! Now I must make sure that the crate is securely tied down. Then you can go to the Cape Town market to deliver this load of fresh fish,' explains Mr. Heavy.

'M-my g-g-goodness!' huffs Larry. 'This crate is r-really

h-heavy! Are you s-sure it won't f-fall off?'

'No. You'll be fine,' Mr. Heavy reassures him.

'W-well, I h-hope I make it there on t-time. This c-crate

could s-slow me down on those hills along

B-boyes D-drive,' stutters Larry.

'Now be careful, Larry.

The roads are very ...'

Larry-Lorry is a little truck that delivers goods around Kalk Bay and Cape Town – sometimes big crates and sometimes small ones.

9

'L-A-R-R-Y! Watch out!' shouts Mr. Heavy.

'W-what on earth …?' Larry exclaims in alarm.

One of Larry-Lorry's back wheels has slipped off the side of the road and is stuck in the mud. He revs his little engine, but he can't move. All he can hear is the spinning of his back wheel. Mud sprays everywhere.

'Oh, n-no. I'm s-stuck!' cries Larry. 'H-how
am I g-going to g-get out of h-here? H-how will I
ever g-g-get to the m-m-market in C-c-cape Town
on t-time? Oh d-deary, d-deary m-me!'

Larry-Lorry is so upset that he stutters more than usual.
He tries once more to move, but the heavy load on
his back prevents him from shifting – even a little bit.

The rain last night has made the ground muddy and slippery. Rain is good for us, but mud can be quite messy.

'Hold on, Larry! We need help.

Where are Maggie and Toby?'

asks Mr. Heavy.

'Toby! Maggie! Where are you?' Mr. Heavy's

voice booms across the harbour.

'We're here,' answers Maggie, the racing yacht, from a

nearby wharf. 'What's the matter?'

'Please hurry. Larry is stuck in the mud and we need your

help,' explains Mr. Heavy.

Maggie and Toby the tugboat make their way across the harbour.

'Now … what to do? What to do?' Mr. Heavy wonders. He scratches his metal head as he plans Larry's rescue.

'What do you want us to do? Just ask. I'll do anything to help,' says Toby.

'Yes, me too. That's what friends are for,' smiles Maggie.

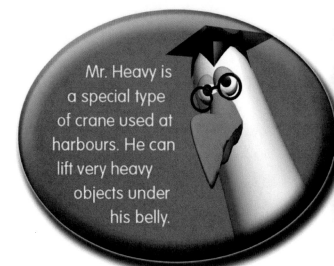

Mr. Heavy is a special type of crane used at harbours. He can lift very heavy objects under his belly.

21

'Larry-Lorry's wheel slipped off the road and now it's completely stuck in the mud. He's very frightened. I tried to lift him out, but my hook is just too big,' Mr. Heavy says.

'Oh, no!' Toby and Maggie cry together.

'I do have a plan, though. I think we can get him out of there, but it'll only work if we work together as a team,' Mr. Heavy explains.

Maggie and Toby nod, eager to help.

22

Mr. Heavy takes a long piece of rope and ties it tightly to the back of Larry-Lorry. Then he pulls the rope through his own hook and hands the end of the rope to Toby and Maggie.

'When I say pull, you must both pull just hard enough to shift Larry out. If you pull too hard,' warns Mr. Heavy, 'he'll land up in the water. Do you understand?'

'Aye aye, Captain,' reply the two boat friends.

'Are you ready, Larry?' calls Mr. Heavy.

Larry wiggles his tail end.

'Okay! All together on the count of three!

One-a-two-a-THREE!' booms

Mr. Heavy.

Toby and Maggie both have strong engines. They should be able to pull Larry out in no time at all.

They pull slowly at first,

to tighten the rope,

then they pull and pull,

and pull some more.

26

'Good work, you two! Larry's moving. Just a little more …

a … l-i-t-t-l-e more! … He's nearly out of the mud,'

coaxes Mr. Heavy. 'Are you okay, Larry?' he calls.

'Y-yes th-thanks!' splutters Larry-Lorry, spitting bits of mud

out of his mouth. He also tries to wipe if off his headlights.

'Come on, Maggie. Just one last tug,' Toby encourages his friend.

Suddenly, they feel the rope move more easily and Larry-Lorry is standing on firm ground. Mud drips from his body.

'Hooray! We did it, we did it!' sing Toby and Maggie, bouncing on the water with glee.

'Well done, you two!' Mr. Heavy congratulates them.

Maggie, Toby, Mr. Heavy and the seagulls look at Larry-Lorry. Then they burst out laughing.

'W-what's the m-m-matter?' asks Larry-Lorry looking rather puzzled.

'You look a mess!' smiles Mr. Heavy. 'You can't go to Cape Town looking like that – covered in mud!'

'Don't worry, Larry!' says Toby. 'I'll sort you out.

Just come a bit closer to the water.' His bell tinkles as he

bobs up and down with excitement.

'W-why?' asks Larry-Lorry. Still

uncertain, he moves closer to

the edge of the jetty.

I have a feeling that Toby is up to something. What do you think?

34

And before Larry realises what's happening ... Toby rushes in towards him.

The next thing Larry feels is a huge wall of clean sea water crashing down on top of him.

'Th-thank you for helping me, m-my friends,' Larry says gratefully. 'And th-thanks, T-t-toby, for my sur-p-p-prise sh-shower. Now I'm n-nice and clean!'

'It's my pleasure,' says Toby smiling.

Revving his little engine, Larry-Lorry carefully drives out of the harbour.

He makes his way along the winding road up the mountain and towards Cape Town.

Do you know what travels along the tracks in this picture?

It's sunset by the time Larry-Lorry returns from the market.

His friends are pleased to see him arriving home safely.

Mr. Heavy calls, 'It's good to see you Larry. Did you have a safe trip?'

'Oh, it was w-w-wonderful,' beams Larry. 'I saw T-table M-mountain again. I r-realised how s-s-small we really are.'

As the skies darken around them, the friends think about all the things that have happened to them during the day.

'It certainly was good to help someone today, wasn't it Maggie?' comments Toby.

'It certainly was. It makes me want to do it more often. What a nice feeling,' sighs Maggie.

'I wonder what tomorrow will bring?' thinks Mr. Heavy out loud.

'W-w-we'll just have to w-wait and see, w-won't we?' says a sleepy Larry-Lorry. 'Thank you, all, for helping me today. You are the best friends ever.'

This was lots of fun. I can't wait for the next story. Do you see how good it is to help someone in need?

In the silence of darkness, Mr. Brightly the lighthouse stands bright-eyed, but he isn't alone. Mr. Moon and the stars are there to keep him company.

46

Made in the USA
Coppell, TX
18 November 2019